Hello, my name is Amarita and this is my mommy Ana!

My mommy has always played a big part in my life. She has always made it clear to me that I can talk to her about anything in the world, no matter how big or small.

My mommy wakes up extra early in the morning to take care of me. First, she does her morning yoga and then she makes us yummy breakfast. Sometimes we have fresh fruit and toast, and other times she makes smoothies to get our day started. My mommy goes to work while I am at school.

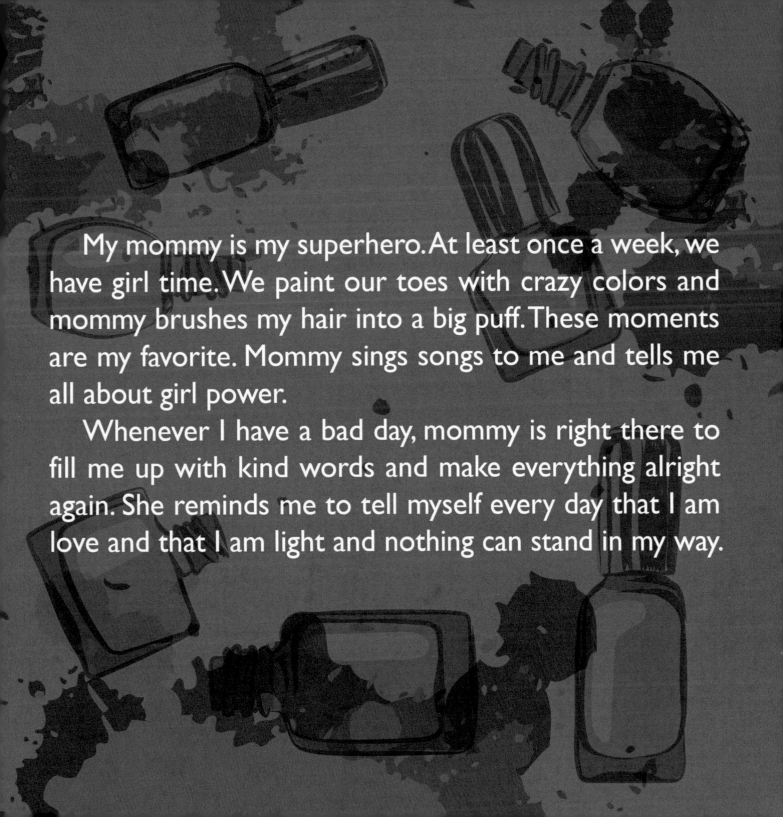

My mommy is my superhero. At least once a week, we have girl time. We paint our toes with crazy colors and mommy brushes my hair into a big puff. These moments are my favorite. Mommy sings songs to me and tells me all about girl power.

Whenever I have a bad day, mommy is right there to fill me up with kind words and make everything alright again. She reminds me to tell myself every day that I am love and that I am light and nothing can stand in my way.

Last Saturday, Mommy took me to the park to have a picnic. The sun was shining bright and the trees blew leaves across the sky. My mommy's curls swished around her face matching the pace of the winds.

She packed our big brown basket with cheese, crackers, fruit and little sandwiches to fill my belly up with nutrients. I sat in the grass and began to roll our big rainbow beach ball around the park.

The sun had finally decided to hide behind the clouds and it started to rain, so we went back home.

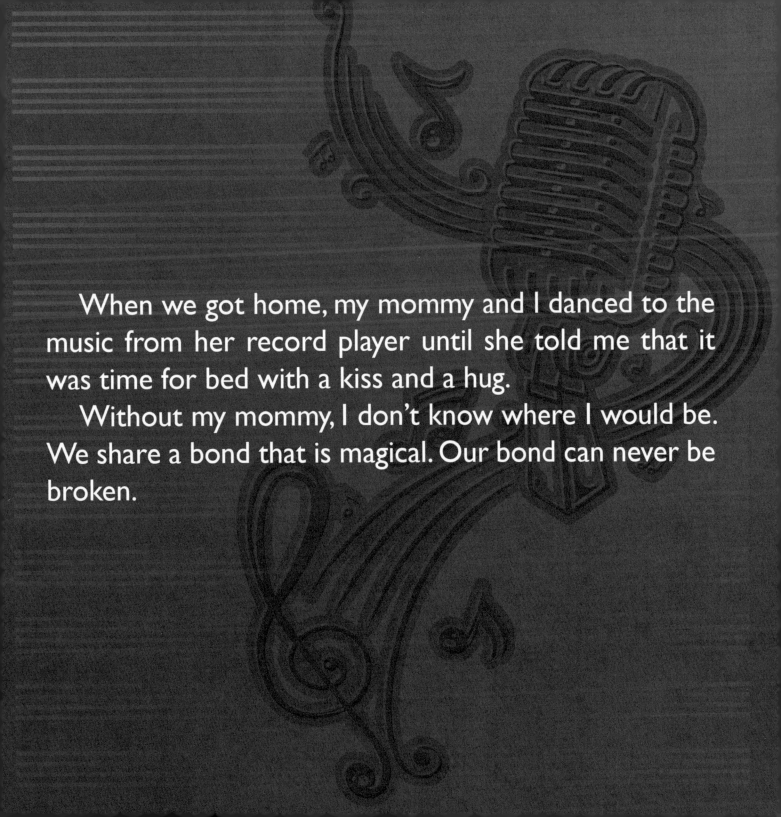

When we got home, my mommy and I danced to the music from her record player until she told me that it was time for bed with a kiss and a hug.

Without my mommy, I don't know where I would be. We share a bond that is magical. Our bond can never be broken.

No matter how hard things get, I never give up. There are times that I get frustrated when I can't accomplish a goal on the first try. My mommy taught me to take deep breathes, count to five, and to keep on trying. She told me that it is extremely important for me to stay determined and focused in everything that I do. It is important not to let anything discourage me from reaching my goals, and to always uplift myself and others in the process.

On our arts and craft days, my mommy would come home with plastic bags filled with art supplies, blank canvasses, and big pieces of white paper to draw on. I knew exactly what I wanted to paint today: A big beautiful rainbow. Mommy gave me my paints, put an apron over my clothes, and gave me a blank canvas. It was time to make my perfect vision come true!

I watched my mommy closely as I worked to copy her motions as she painted a big yellow sunflower. My rainbow had gotten a little smudged but I tried to fix it by adding some more red paint to the outside of the rainbow. I glanced over at my mommy's sunflower and it was perfect! She added big yellow and brown petals and started working on the stem. I took a deep breath and walked away from my painting, leaving the imperfectly smudged rainbow to sit alone. I tossed the apron on the floor and went to my room.

I heard my mommy's footsteps approaching my room.

"What's going on Amarita, why'd you leave your pretty picture unfinished?" she asked.

"I messed up, it's ugly and I don't want to finish it mommy," I said.

"Amarita, it has so much potential, we can fix it up. Let's work on it together," she smiled.

"I'm done with it mommy, I messed it all up!" I said as tears welled up in my eyes.

My mommy walked closer to me and looked me in the eye.

"You cannot give up just because you made a little mistake. You must keep going, you have to be determined in every single thing that you do," my mommy said with a serious look on her face.

"Okay mommy. I'll try to fix the painting," I said.

"This is much deeper than the painting, baby, you have to be determined in everything that you take on in life. Finish what you start," she said.

I went back into the living room and corrected my mistakes. I ended up with a big beautiful rainbow! From that day on, I have decided to finish everything that I start and show determination in everything that I do. I never give up on myself, instead, I keep going. That's the Amarita way!

My mommy always told me that self-love is the purest and most important kind of love. She told me that if I was able to love myself in this world, I would be able to do anything. Sometimes it can be hard, especially with this society's high standard of beauty, but she told me to always remember that I am beautiful.

One day before picture day at school, my mommy rubbed warm coconut oil in my hair and brushed it out into a big afro. She put two pink barrettes in the front of my hair, and picked out a pink dress to match. Mommy smiled so big when she saw how pretty I looked before I left for the school bus.

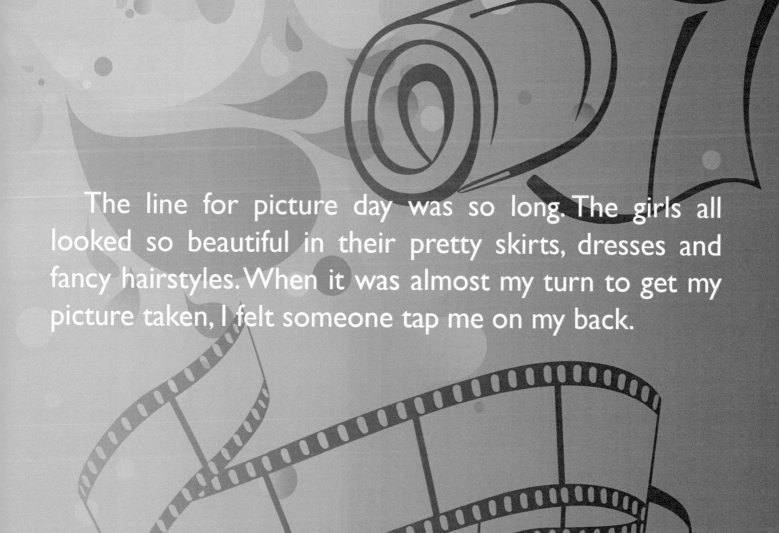

The line for picture day was so long. The girls all looked so beautiful in their pretty skirts, dresses and fancy hairstyles. When it was almost my turn to get my picture taken, I felt someone tap me on my back.

I turned around and, to my surprise, it was Samantha Baker. Samantha Baker was usually quiet but when she had a question about something, she wouldn't hesitate to ask.

"Amarita, why is your hair all over your head like that?" asked Samantha.

My thoughts were racing through my head, but I could remember my mommy telling me exactly how to respond in moments like these. She would tell me not to get mad or offended but to educate them instead.

"It's called an afro, it literally defies gravity, pretty cool huh?" I asked and walked away to take my picture.

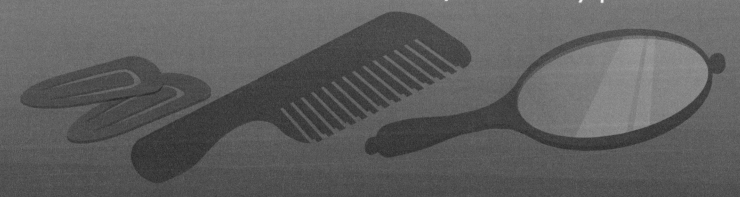

My mommy taught me that self-love should not be put in the same category as arrogance. Self-love isn't selfishness; it's something that you owe to yourself.

We should all love ourselves unconditionally and learn to embrace our "flaws". Flaws are really just differences that set us apart from everyone else and are nothing to be ashamed of.

My mommy always said that self-love should be taught to children at the same time as the ABC's so that they won't have to learn it later on in life.

I will always love myself unconditionally, and you should too. It's the Amarita way.

VISIT
WWW.MCBRIDESTORIES.COM
FOR MORE TITLES

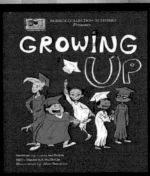

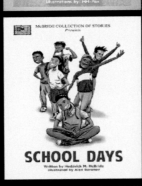

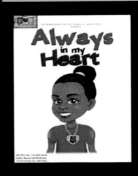

33960917R00020

Made in the USA
Middletown, DE
27 January 2019